The Cat Who Walked by Himself

Retold by Elizabeth Rogers

Illustrated by O'Kif

FRANKLIN WATTS

First published in 2010 by
Franklin Watts
338 Euston Road
London
NW1 3BH

Franklin Watts Australia
Level 17/207 Kent Street
Sydney
NSW 2000

Text © Franklin Watts 2010
Illustration © O'Kif 2010

The rights of Elizabeth Rogers to be identified as the
author and O'Kif as the illustrator of this Work
have been asserted in accordance with the Copyright,
Designs and Patents Act, 1988.

A CIP catalogue record for this book is available
from the British Library.

ISBN 978 0 7496 9403 6 (hbk)
ISBN 978 0 7496 9409 8 (pbk)

Series Editor: Jackie Hamley
Series Advisor: Catherine Glavina
Series Designer: Peter Scoulding

Printed in China

Franklin Watts is a division of
Hachette Children's Books,
an Hachette UK company.
www.hachette.co.uk

This Just So story is
based on a tale written
by an author called
Rudyard Kipling over
a hundred years ago.

Just So stories give fun
ideas for why different
animals are like they are.

Long ago, the animals saw people's fire.

"I'll find out what that is," said Dog.

"I won't," said Cat.
"I walk by myself!"

Soon, Horse went to find Dog.

"I'm not going," said
Cat. "I walk by myself!"

Next day, Cat went
to the people's cave.

"Go away, Cat who walks by himself!" said the woman.

"But it looks warm," said Cat.

"If I'm nice to you three times, you can come in," said the woman.

11

Later, the woman's baby was crying ... until Cat played a game with him.

Then the baby would not sleep ... until Cat purred to him.

15

A mouse ran up ...
and Cat caught it.

Suddenly, Cat was in the cave, by the fire, with a bowl of milk.

19

And so the Cat who walked by himself made friends with people!

21

Puzzle Time!

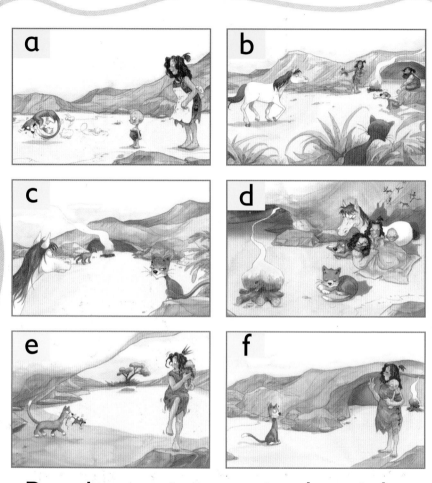

Put these pictures in the right order and tell the story!

Notes for adults

TADPOLES are structured to provide support for newly independent readers. The stories may also be used by adults for sharing with young children.

Starting to read alone can be daunting. **TADPOLES** help by providing visual support and repeating words and phrases. These books will both develop confidence and encourage reading and rereading for pleasure.

If you are reading this book with a child, here are a few suggestions:

1. Make reading fun! Choose a time to read when you and the child are relaxed and have time to share the story.
2. Talk about the story before you start reading. Look at the cover and the blurb. What might the story be about? Why might the child like it?
3. Encourage the child to retell the story, using the jumbled picture puzzle as a starting point. Extend vocabulary with the matching words to characters puzzle.
4. Talk about how the story has fun with cats' independent natures, and see if you can think of other animals and why they might look or behave the way they do.
5. Give praise! Remember that small mistakes need not always be corrected.

Answers

Here is the correct order:
1. c 2. b 3. f 4. a 5. e 6. d

Words to describe the cat:
bold, free

Words to describe the woman:
angry, cross

bold

angry

free

cross

Which words describe the cat
and which describe the woman?

Turn over for answers!